1001
Things to Spot in the Town

Anna Milbourne
Illustrated by Teri Gower

Designed by Susannah Owen

Edited by Gillian Doherty
Series editor: Felicity Brooks   Series designer: Mary Cartwright

Additional design: Nicola Butler
Cover design: Helen Wood

Contents

Things to spot

The pictures in this book show scenes from different towns. On every page there are lots of things for you to find and count.

There are 1001 things to spot altogether. The example pages below show what you need to do to find them.

Each little picture shows you what to look for in the big picture.

The blue number tells you how many of that thing you need to find.

This is Sam. She visited each of the towns in the book. See if you can spot her in each scene.

Sam took photos of her trip and she brought things back from each town. On pages 30 and 31 you can look at these things and there are two puzzles for you to do.

3

Street café

3 newspapers

6 trays

8 pieces of cake

7 waiters

10 glasses of juice

9 pigeons

6 parasols

5 ice creams

10 menus

1 musician

Market town

4 donkeys

10 red rugs

8 sacks of spices

10 blue bowls

7 lanterns

6

9 crates of oranges

2 snakes

3 carts

7 teapots

6 mirrors

Nightlife

9 blue caps

3 hot dog stands

10 cartons of popcorn

4 yellow taxis

6 street lights

1 ticket seller
8 drinks with straws
1 girl running
3 burger signs
10 umbrellas

River town

8 baskets of bananas

7 washing lines

2 pots of red flowers

5 tubs of laundry

4 monks

1 ferry

10 straw hats

7 children splashing

6 baskets of rice

9 baskets of peppers

Town square

1 fountain

7 pink arches

10 school bags

9 pigeons flying

4 street artists

10 scooters

1 clock

10 ice creams

4 banners

7 piles of books

Fortress town

3 camels

10 orange turbans

3 elephants

8 bowls of samosas

10 women in pink saris

10 sacks

8 cows

9 flower garlands

1 gateway

10 blue books

Town park

2 kites

3 swings

9 ducklings

8 soccer players

2 red boats

10 red tulips

8 dogs

5 benches

8 squirrels

6 people
skating

Traffic jam

8 green taxis

2 road signs

10 bicycles

3 buses

9 brown briefcases

10 school boys

2 trucks

8 blue cars

1 street barber

2 bus stops

Fishing port

8 cats
5 empty buckets
10 seagulls
7 crab pots
3 nets

9 crabs

10 buckets of fish

6 fishermen

2 postcard stands

4 boats

Country village

9 buckets of water

10 soccer players

8 babies in slings

9 women pounding grain

4 children with hoops

9 dishes of mangoes

1 well

10 goats

7 huts

9 striped headscarves

Shopping street

9 skateboards
7 shoeboxes
8 striped T-shirts
10 beach balls
6 swimsuits

9 toy kangaroos   6 jars of lollipops   8 flowery dresses   10 red bags   8 kookaburras

Snowy town

10 blue parkas

1 plane

10 dogs

9 log cabins

5 snowmobiles

6 ravens

4 green sleighs

10 boxes

9 striped hats

2 moose

Carnival

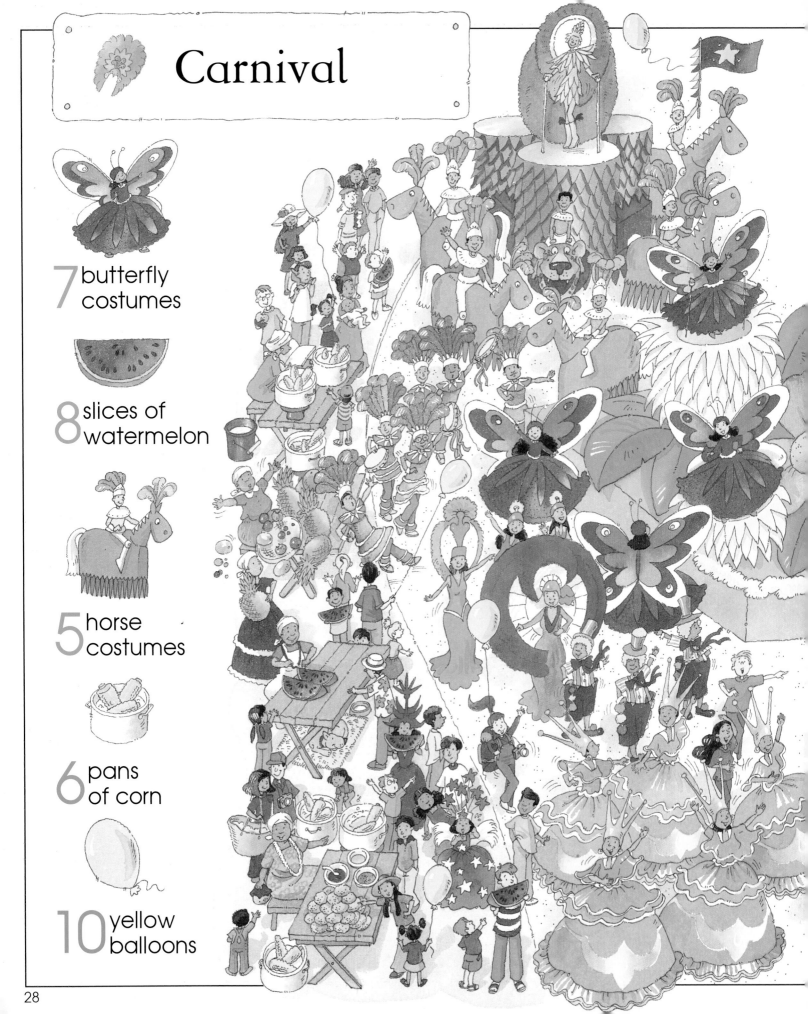

7 butterfly costumes

8 slices of watermelon

5 horse costumes

6 pans of corn

10 yellow balloons

9 gold crowns   6 drummers   4 pineapples   10 flags   8 clowns

Photos

These are photos that Sam took in the towns she went to. Can you find which scene each photo is from?

Souvenirs

Sam brought these souvenirs back from the towns she visited. Can you find which towns they are from and count them all?

10 blue and white teapots

10 striped bags

4 posters of aliens

10 yellow shells

9 wooden elephants

8 orange feathers

10 brown fur hats

7 starfish

4 boxes of chocolates

9 yellow rugs

5 cake boxes

10 balloons with faces

3 koras

9 napkins

2 paper boats

9 puppets

Answers

Did you find all the photos and the souvenirs throughout the book? Here's where they are.

Photos

1 Carnival
   (page 29)

2 Town park
   (page 17)

3 River town
   (page 10)

4 Street café
   (page 5)

5 Market town
   (page 7)

6 Fortress town
   (page 14)

7 Nightlife
   (page 9)

8 Fishing port
   (page 21)

9 Town square
   (page 13)

10 Traffic jam
   (page 19)

11 Snowy town
   (page 26)

12 Shopping street
   (page 24)

13 Country village
   (page 22)

Souvenirs

10 blue and white teapots:
   Traffic jam
   (pages 18 and 19)

10 striped bags:
   Shopping street
   (pages 24 and 25)

4 posters of aliens:
   Nightlife
   (pages 8 and 9)

10 yellow shells:
   Fishing port
   (pages 20 and 21)

9 wooden elephants:
   River town
   (pages 10 and 11)

8 orange feathers:
   Carnival
   (pages 28 and 29)

10 brown fur hats:
   Snowy town
   (pages 26 and 27)

7 starfish:
   Fishing port
   (pages 20 and 21)

4 boxes of chocolates:
   Street café
   (pages 4 and 5)

9 yellow rugs:
   Market town
   (pages 6 and 7)

5 cake boxes:
   Street café
   (pages 4 and 5)

10 balloons with faces:
   Town square
   (pages 12 and 13)

3 koras:
   Country village
   (pages 22 and 23)

9 napkins:
   Street café
   (pages 4 and 5)

2 paper boats:
   Town park
   (pages 16 and 17)

9 puppets:
   Fortress town
   (pages 14 and 15)

Acknowledgements

The publishers would like to thank the following people for providing information about different towns:

Caroline Liou, China
Cheryl Ward, Australia
Daryl Bowers, Barrow, Alaska
Mr Jensen, Dan Fishing
Equipment Ltd., Denmark
Frances Linzee Gordon, Morocco
Helene Kratzsch and Marie Rose
von Wesendonk
Ibrahim Keith Holt, The Council of
the Obsidian, West Africa Office
Imogen Franks, Lonely Planet Publications
Michael Willis, Curator, British Museum
Susannah Selwyn, ES International
Language Schools